Sam the Man & the Cell Phone Plan

Also by Frances O'Roark Dowell

Anybody Shining
Chicken Boy
Dovey Coe
Falling In
The Second Life of Abigail Walker
Shooting the Moon
Ten Miles Past Normal
Trouble the Water
Where I'd Like to Be

The Secret Language of Girls Trilogy
The Secret Language of Girls
The Kind of Friends We Used to Be
The Sound of Your Voice, Only Really Far Away

From the Highly Scientific Notebooks of
Phineas L. MacGuire
Phineas L. MacGuire . . . Blasts Off!
Phineas L. MacGuire . . . Erupts!
Phineas L. MacGuire . . . Gets Cooking!
Phineas L. MacGuire . . . Gets Slimed!

The Sam the Man series
#1: Sam the Man & the Chicken Plan
#2: Sam the Man & the Rutabaga Plan
#3: Sam the Man & the Dragon Van Plan
#4: Sam the Man & the Secret Detective Club Plan

SAM THE MAN 5:

SAM THE MAN

& the Cell Phone Plan

FRANCES O'ROARK DOWELL

Illustrated by **Amy June Bates**

A Caitlyn Dlouhy Book

 Atheneum Books for Young Readers
New York London Toronto Sydney New Delhi

ATHENEUM BOOKS FOR YOUNG READERS

An imprint of Simon & Schuster Children's Publishing Division

1230 Avenue of the Americas, New York, New York 10020

This book is a work of fiction. Any references to historical events, real people, or real places are used fictitiously. Other names, characters, places, and events are products of the author's imagination, and any resemblance to actual events or places or persons, living or dead, is entirely coincidental.

Text copyright © 2019 by Frances O'Roark Dowell

Illustrations copyright © 2019 by Amy June Bates

All rights reserved, including the right of reproduction in whole or in part in any form.

ATHENEUM BOOKS FOR YOUNG READERS is a registered trademark of Simon & Schuster, Inc. Atheneum logo is a trademark of Simon & Schuster, Inc.

For information about special discounts for bulk purchases, please contact Simon & Schuster Special Sales at 1-866-506-1949 or business@simonandschuster.com.

The Simon & Schuster Speakers Bureau can bring authors to your live event. For more information or to book an event, contact the Simon & Schuster Speakers Bureau at 1-866-248-3049 or visit our website at www.simonspeakers.com.

Book design by Sonia Chaghatzbanian and Irene Metaxatos

The text for this book was set in New Century Schoolbook LT Std.

The illustrations for this book were rendered in pencil.

Manufactured in the United States of America

1019 FFG

First Edition

10 9 8 7 6 5 4 3 2

Library of Congress Cataloging-in-Publication Data

Names: Dowell, Frances O'Roark, author. | Bates, Amy June, illustrator.

Title: Sam the Man & the cell phone plan / Frances O'Roark Dowell ; illustrated by Amy June Bates.

Other titles: Sam the Man and the cell phone plan

Description: First edition. | New York : Atheneum Books for Young Readers, [2019] | "A Caitlyn Dlouhy Book." | Summary: Second-grader Sam Graham wants a cell phone to do research and share information but when his parents say no, he devises a new plan that starts a fad at school.

Identifiers: LCCN 2018034266| ISBN 9781534412613 (hardcover) | ISBN 9781534412637 (eBook)

Subjects: | CYAC: Notebooks—Fiction. | Ciphers—Fiction. | Schools—Fiction. | Cell phones—Fiction. | Family life—Fiction.

Classification: LCC PZ7.D75455 Sag 2019 | DDC [Fic]—dc23 LC record available at https://lccn.loc.gov/2018034266

Chapter One

Sam "Just the Facts" Graham

S am Graham was an information man.

In his room he had three books about chickens, seven books about monster trucks, one copy of *Guinness World Records*, and a comic book called *Everything You Need to Know About the Solar System*.

When his second-grade class went to the library, Sam helped the other kids look things up on the computer. He helped

Emily find websites about bird calls, and he helped Will look up statistics on his favorite college football team. When Sam needed facts about his favorite food group, he knew the best thing to type into the search engine box was "frozen waffles history," because if he just typed "frozen waffles," all the hits would be commercials, and commercials never had facts in them.

Sam liked facts. He liked researching facts about interesting topics. He liked sharing the facts he learned with other people.

Which is why Sam Graham needed his very own phone.

"A phone? Why on earth does a second grader need a phone?" Sam's mom asked when Sam told her what he wanted for his birthday. She was sitting at the breakfast table, reading the newspaper on her laptop computer.

"I like looking things up," Sam said, taking a bite of his frozen waffle. "It would be nice if I could look up stuff while I was on the school bus or taking care of the chickens in Mrs. Kerner's backyard. And if I had a phone and there was a chicken emergency, I could call 9-1-1."

"You don't call 9-1-1 for chickens, Sam the Man," Sam's sister, Annabelle, told him. "You'd get in trouble if you did."

"Well, I could call you or Mom or Dad, then," Sam said. "Or the chicken hotline."

"Is there really a chicken hotline?"

Sam's mom asked, looking over her computer screen at Sam and Annabelle.

"If I had a phone, I could look it up and see," Sam said.

Annabelle took out her phone from her back pocket. "I'll check."

"No phones at the table, Annabelle," Sam's mom said. "You know the rules."

"But you have your laptop at the table," Annabelle pointed out. "That's almost the same as a phone."

"In this case, my laptop is really a newspaper," Sam's mom said. "So it's different."

"If I had a phone, I could read the paper too," Sam said. "My phone could be a newspaper or a book or an encyclopedia or a radio."

Sam's dad walked into the kitchen. He

4

had his phone in his hand and was texting someone.

"And I could text you if I had to stay late for school or needed to come home because I had a stomachache," Sam continued. "I could do a million things with a phone."

"You're too young for a phone, Sam the Man," Sam's dad said, putting *his* phone on the kitchen counter. "You spend too much time looking at screens as it is."

Sam poured some more syrup on his frozen waffle. "Why isn't Annabelle too young?" he asked.

"Annabelle is in sixth grade," Sam's dad said. "She has Scouts and soccer and swim team. She also has asthma, so it makes me and your mom feel better to know she can get in touch with us if she feels an attack coming on while she's at school or a game."

"Besides, Sam, you have lots of ways to look things up," Sam's mom added, closing her laptop and taking her plate to the sink. "You can use the computer in my office upstairs if I'm there to supervise, and you can always check out books from the

library. You don't need a phone to find things out."

Sam thought about this. He knew there were lots of ways to look up facts. But he couldn't take pictures using a book, and he couldn't pull his mom's computer out of his

pocket if he needed to send someone a message. And what was he supposed to do if he had a chicken coop emergency? Throw eggs up into the air and hope someone came to see what was the matter?

But he could tell from their expressions that his parents weren't going to get him a phone for his birthday, even if it *was* the best idea ever. The problem, Sam thought as he scrubbed syrup off his arm with his napkin, was now all he could think about was how much he wanted a phone. How much he *needed* a phone. How he would never be happy until the day he finally had a phone of his own.

There was only one thing to do. Sam would have to come up with a plan.

He tried to come up with one while he was brushing his teeth. Maybe he could ask Annabelle if he could rent her phone part time, even though he knew she'd probably say no. Annabelle was the kind of sister who would help you out, but she wouldn't break the rules for you.

He could look in the school lost and found to see if anyone had lost a phone. Sure, he'd have to give the phone back to its owner, but maybe that person would be so happy that Sam had found their phone, they'd let Sam use it whenever he wanted. They might even let Sam bring it home on the weekends.

Sam liked that plan a lot, but his parents probably wouldn't.

By the time Sam had finished brushing his teeth, put on his jacket, and walked to the bus stop, he'd thought of six different plans, but he was pretty sure none of them would work.

Sam wasn't used to coming up with bad plans. It made him feel dumb. It was like when he played T-ball last spring and kept hitting the tee instead of the ball when it was his turn to bat.

"You look sad, Sam," Sam's best friend, Gavin, said when he got to the bus stop. "Did you lose something?"

Sam shook his head. "I'm trying to come up with a plan for getting a phone, but I can't think of anything good."

"No one in second grade has a phone," Gavin said. "Well, Hutch did for a little while, remember? His mom put tracking devices in his jacket and lunch box because Hutch was always losing them. He was supposed to use the phone to track his lost stuff."

"But he lost the phone," Sam said, nodding. "I remember."

"I don't think you need a phone," Gavin said. "But if you really want one, you could tell your parents you'd pay for it. You're good at making money."

"I still don't think they'd let me have one," Sam said.

"So then why are you trying to come up with a plan to get one?" Gavin asked.

Sam saw the bus coming down the street and picked up his backpack. "I don't know. I just really want a phone."

"I feel the same way about cats," Gavin said, lining up with Sam for the bus. "I really, really want a cat. But I'm allergic to cats, and so is everybody else in my family. So I'm never going to have a cat, even though I want one more than anything."

"No one is my family is allergic to phones," Sam said. "In fact, I'm the only person who doesn't have one. It's not fair."

"Life's not fair," Gavin said as they stepped onto the bus. "Otherwise I wouldn't have a cat allergy."

"I guess," Sam said. He was about to say something else when he slipped on a piece of paper on the bus floor. He didn't fall, but he did bump into the boy in front of him.

The boy turned around and said, "Watch it!" He was carrying a box, which he showed to Sam. "I made a robot for the third-grade science fair, and I don't want to break it."

"Sorry," Sam said. He wished he could peek inside the box to see what the boy's robot looked like. He wondered if it would be hard to make a robot, one that walked and talked and did all kinds of interesting things. Maybe next year Sam would make his own robot for the science fair.

Or—

Sam turned around to Gavin. "I've got it! I've come up with a plan!"

"What is it?" Gavin asked.

"I'm going to make my own phone!" Sam told him. "It's going to be great!"

"Make a phone?" Gavin sounded confused. "How do you *make* a phone?"

Sam shrugged. "I don't know. But I know how to look it up."

If there was one thing Sam was good at, it was looking things up.

Chapter Two

How to Make a Phone of Your Own

"I've never heard of anyone making a phone," Mr. Stockfish said. "Well, except for Alexander Graham Bell. Oh, and my brother, Archie. He used tin cans and a piece of string."

"Did it work?" Sam asked.

"Not really, but we pretended it did." Mr. Stockfish glanced at the chicken in his lap. "Do you think Leroy's eyes look funny today?"

Sam and Mr. Stockfish were sitting by the chicken coop in their neighbor's backyard, which they did most afternoons. Mrs. Kerner had a flock of chickens that Sam took care of. Sam also took care of his own chicken, Helga, and Leroy, who belonged to Mr. Stockfish. Spending time with Leroy in Mrs. Kerner's backyard was one of Mr. Stockfish's favorite things to do.

Sam leaned over and looked at Leroy. "Her eyes might be a little more yellow today than usual, but that's probably just because the leaves in the trees are turning yellow."

"You think Leroy's eye color is affected by the color of the leaves?"

"My mom says that when I wear my blue shirt, my eyes look more blue," Sam

16

explained. "Usually they look gray."

Mr. Stockfish looked at Leroy's eyes more closely. "Maybe you're right, Sam. Maybe it is the leaves. She's not acting sick."

"She's moving around a lot and seems like she's interested in our conversation," Sam said. "I think if she was sick, she would seem more bored. If I had a phone, I could look up how to tell if a chicken is sick."

"But you already know," Mr. Stockfish pointed out. "You just told me."

"I don't know for sure," Sam argued. "I just know from spending a lot of time with healthy chickens how a healthy chicken looks."

"How much time do you think a phone has spent with healthy chickens?" Mr.

Stockfish asked. "Or any chickens at all?"

"If I had a phone, I could ask it," Sam said. "Phones have little voices in them that can tell you things."

"Your brain has a little voice in it that can tell you things too," Mr. Stockfish pointed out. "It sounds like it might even be able to tell you how to make your own phone."

"I learned about how to make a phone by searching the Internet," Sam said. "First I have to get all the right ingredients. You need, um—" Sam paused and pulled a small notebook out of his back pocket. "I made a list. You need something called 'indium tin oxide' for the screen and small amounts of rare earths. Do you know what rare earths are? I didn't have time to look that up."

"Rare earths are metals," Mr. Stockfish said. "They're used to make computers."

"I bet my mom could order some online," Sam said. "Plus a battery, because phones use batteries."

Mr. Stockfish patted Leroy on the head. He seemed to be thinking. After a moment he said, "Sam, you have your brain and a notebook. You're good at looking things up. I don't understand why you need a phone. You already have everything a phone has."

"I don't have a camera," Sam said, pretending to take a picture of Leroy by clicking an invisible button on an invisible phone.

"Your eyes are a camera," Mr. Stockfish said. "They take pictures that you keep in your memory."

"I don't have a keypad to type texts on," Sam said. He tapped a message on the palm of his hand. "I have fingers, but no keypad."

"You have a notebook and a pencil," Mr. Stockfish said.

"I don't have a whole library of information," Sam said.

"You have your brain," Mr. Stockfish said. "And the ability to think. You didn't need a phone to convince me that Leroy is healthy."

"A phone knows a lot more than my brain does," Sam said. "But I have to stop arguing with you now because I need to fill up the chickens' waterer."

"See, you didn't need a phone to tell you that," Mr. Stockfish said. "All you needed was your eyes and your experience."

"Okay, okay," Sam said, ducking into the coop with the hose. "I get it. But I'm still going to try to make my own phone."

"Nothing wrong with that, Sam," Mr. Stockfish said as he put Leroy on the ground. "I'll go turn the water on for you."

Sam put the end of the hose into the waterer's top. "Ready!" he called to Mr. Stockfish. "I'll tell you when to turn the water off. And please don't say that a phone couldn't tell you when to do that."

"Okay, I won't say it," Mr. Stockfish said. "But it's true."

Sam listened to the waterer going *glug glug glug* as the water from the hose filled it up. He thought about all the different things he would need to make his own phone. He knew that phone cases were made out of aluminum, and they

21

had aluminum foil in the kitchen drawer next to the stove. But was that the right kind of aluminum? He also knew that if he wanted to use his phone to talk or to listen to monster truck podcasts he would need a speaker, but he wasn't sure how you made a speaker. Maybe he could use aluminum foil for that, too.

Sam pulled out his notebook again to check his notes. He would need to make something called a processor chip. For that you needed silicon, and Sam wasn't sure what silicon was. He didn't know what micro-capacitors were, either, but phones needed those, too.

Don't worry about it, Sam told himself. He could look everything up. He was good at looking things up, remember?

But then Sam had a terrible thought.

Supplies List

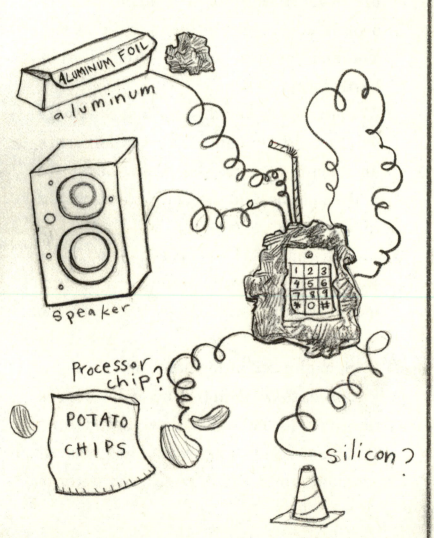

ALUMINUM FOIL

aluminum

speaker

Processor chip?

POTATO CHIPS

silicon?

What if he looked everything up, figured everything out, and made his very own phone . . . and his mom and dad still wouldn't let him use it? After all that hard work!

Sam shook his head. That's exactly what would happen. He'd work for hours and hours—maybe even for days!—to make a phone, and then his parents would take it away.

But what was he supposed to do? Make a phone his parents wouldn't mind him using? What would that kind of phone even look like?

Sam glanced at his notebook. He knew his parents wouldn't mind if he used a notebook. If he wrote down everything that he needed to know in a notebook, it might sort of be like having a computer in his pocket. After all, he knew a whole lot.

What else? His mom had an old digital camera that she never used anymore. Maybe she'd let Sam have it. That could be kind of like having a phone with a camera in it. He just wouldn't have the phone part.

But what if Sam needed to make an actual phone call? What if he needed to send somebody a message?

He would need some sort of message machine. And he would need . . . he would need . . . he would need a secret code! Yes, Sam would need a secret code and a way to send it.

"Sam, I think the waterer is filled up now," Mr. Stockfish called. "In fact, it looks like the water is spilling over the top."

Sam looked down. Not only was the

waterer filled up, but water was spilling out and his shoes were wet. "Okay, I guess you could turn off the hose now," he called to Mr. Stockfish.

Sam pulled the hose out of the coop and coiled it back up. When he was done putting it away, he went to sit in the lawn chair next to Mr. Stockfish.

"Do you know anything about secret codes?" he asked.

Mr. Stockfish bent down and scooped Leroy back into his lap. "Of course I do. I used to be in the army, and working with codes was part of my job."

Sam leaned back in his seat and smiled. He was pretty sure he'd just come up with a brand-new plan.

Chapter Three

Sam the Man and the Secret Code Plan

When Sam got home, he went upstairs to his mom's office. "I need to do some research," he said after knocking on the door. "Can I use your computer?"

"Come on in, Sam," his mom said. She was sitting at her desk, typing on her desktop computer, which had a humongous screen and a keyboard that you plugged into the back. "My laptop is over by the chair. What are you going to look up?"

Sam thought about what he should say. When you were looking up secret codes, should you keep it a secret? He guessed it was okay to tell his mom, who would probably come over and look anyway. Sam's mom was very nosy when Sam was using the computer.

"Mr. Stockfish said that when he was in the army, he helped send secret messages using special codes." Sam sat down in the chair across the room from his mom and picked up her laptop. "He also said that there were codes that weren't secret. Did you know the army has its own alphabet?"

Sam's mom turned around to look at Sam. "I think so. 'Alpha, Bravo, Charlie' is *A*, *B*, *C*, right?"

"Yep," Sam said. "And *D* is 'Delta.' But I forget after that."

"You could probably find some codes on the Internet that you could print out," Sam's mom said.

Sam thought that was a good plan. In fact, he could make his own code book. Then he would have a lot of different ways to send messages to his friends. They'd have to know the codes too, but Sam could make them copies of the code book.

Sam found an Internet site that had a bunch of codes that kids could use. Some of them he didn't understand, but there were a few that were really cool. There was one where you gave each letter of the alphabet a number, so that *A* was zero, and *B* was one, and *C* was two, etc. When you needed to send a message, you wrote it out in numbers instead of letters, so that nobody but your friends who knew the code could read it.

When Sam was done printing out all the codes he wanted to try, he stapled the pages together and took them to Annabelle's room. Annabelle was sitting on her bed, untangling the knots in the laces of her soccer cleats.

"That looks like a cool book," Annabelle said after Sam showed her what he'd just done. "But I guess there's one thing I don't understand. Why do you have to send messages in code? When I text my friends, I don't text them in code."

"But when your friends text you back, the only person who can see the texts is you," Sam said. "Because you keep your phone in your pocket, right? And then when you get a text, you take your phone out of your pocket and look at it. It's not like someone leaves their phone on your desk so you can read the message they sent you. But if you pass someone a piece of paper . . ."

"Someone might grab it and read it," Annabelle finished. "I had that happen to me once."

"What was the note about?" Sam asked.

"Soccer practice, so it wasn't a big deal," Annabelle said, tugging at her shoelace to make the last knot come out. "Still, it made me really mad when Zeph Bamberger grabbed the note and read it out loud to everybody."

"That would make me mad too," Sam agreed. He was glad Annabelle understood why he wanted to use secret codes instead of regular words for his messages. Sometimes when Sam came up with ideas he thought were good, someone else would point out why they weren't good at all, and then Sam had to come up with a whole new idea. It was kind of exhausting.

Sam took the pages back to his room and put them on his desk next to his notebook. He wished there were a better way to send messages than just writing them down on pieces of paper. That seemed pretty boring. But what else was there, if you didn't have a phone to send messages with? Sam had heard about pigeons that carried messages back and forth between people, but how practical was that? First you'd have to find a pigeon, and then you'd have to train a pigeon to fly from your house to all your friends' houses, and that could take forever. Plus, what if the pigeon got tired of carrying messages all day and decided to fly away?

Probably the best thing to do was to start with paper, even if paper was boring. After he and his friends had learned to write to one another in code, they could figure out more interesting ways to send messages back and forth. Sam wondered if anyone ever used squirrels to carry messages. He'd actually never seen a pigeon in his neighborhood, but squirrels were everywhere.

Sam looked at his little notebook. He liked how it was sort of shaped like a phone. The spiral wire that held the notebook together was at the top instead of

33

the side, which made the notebook easier to slide into his pocket. Maybe people
who saw it would think it actually *was*
a phone. Sam liked that idea. In fact, he
liked it so much he got another great idea
right away.

Sam put his notebook in his back
pocket and went downstairs to his dad's
office, which was really a storage space
next to the kitchen that Sam's family
didn't store anything in. Instead there
was a card table where Sam's dad worked
on his laptop. There was also a shelf with
papers and the computer magazines
Sam's dad liked to read.

Looking through the stack of magazines, Sam found an old one he thought
would be okay to use. It didn't take him
long to find an ad that had a picture of a

smart phone. The picture was bigger than Sam's notebook, but Sam knew how to fix that. He went into the kitchen to grab a pair of scissors from the junk drawer and then very carefully cut out the picture so it was the right size. Then he got a glue stick from the junk drawer and glued the picture to the front of his notebook.

There were good things and bad things about the picture, Sam thought while he waited for the glue to dry. One of the bad things was that the phone had the time on its screen. It read 12:45. But if Sam took his notebook out of his pocket at 2:33, everyone would think it was strange that his phone said 12:45. Sam guessed he would just say that his phone's clock was broken. Or else that he had it on army time, which was different from regular time. Mr. Stockfish had told Sam that, and Sam wasn't sure what he meant, but that was okay. Nobody else would either.

One of the good things was that the phone screen had little pictures on it, like a picture of a camera and another one of a little globe. Sam knew the little globe was a symbol for the Internet. So whenever he needed to look up a fact in his notebook, he just had to remember to tap the little globe first.

When he was pretty sure the glue was dry and the picture was stuck to the notebook, Sam practiced putting his notebook into his pocket, pulling it out, and tapping on the cover. Yes! It worked perfectly.

Now all Sam had to do was fill his notebook with information. And he also needed to write Gavin a message in secret code. He wished there was a way to send messages that seemed more like he was sending real texts. Maybe all of his friends could get notebooks like Sam's. Then they could write their messages in their notebooks and pass them around. Sam would have to get another notebook, because he wouldn't want to pass his information notebook around. But that was okay, because Sam really liked little notebooks. Also, it would look like he had *two* phones.

Sam took his notebook upstairs and got one of his books about monster trucks out of his bookcase. He sat down at his desk and opened his notebook to the first blank page and opened the monster truck book to its first page.

A monster truck is a very large pickup truck with very big tires, Sam wrote in his notebook. *You can go to monster truck shows and watch the monster trucks run over small cars. Monster trucks are the best kind of trucks.*

Sam looked up and smiled. When he got his notebook filled up with information, it would be even better than a phone.

He couldn't wait.

Chapter Four

Code Busters

"I thought you said your parents wouldn't let you have a phone?"

Gavin pointed at the notebook in Sam's hand and shook his head. "I mean, didn't you say they were allergic to phones?"

"No, I didn't say that," Sam said, trying not to giggle. Gavin really thought his notebook was a phone! "You said *your* family is allergic to cats."

"Oh, right," Gavin said. "That's different from your parents being allergic to phones. But you *did* say you weren't allowed to have a phone. So where'd you get that one?"

Sam leaned closer to Gavin on the school bus seat and held his notebook right in front of his face. "It's not really a phone. It's a notebook I made to look like a phone." He opened up the notebook to show Gavin what he'd written in it so far. "Right now you can use it to find out facts about monster trucks and chickens, but pretty soon it's going to have everything in it."

"Everything?" Gavin sounded doubtful. "Everything is a lot of things."

"It will have everything that's interesting," Sam told him. "So it probably won't have, like, different types of grass you can grow in your backyard or stuff like that. But if you want to know about frozen waffles, you can find it here."

"I like frozen waffles," Gavin said, nodding. "And I'd be interested to know more about them."

"I almost forgot!" Sam said, opening up his backpack. "I have something to give you."

"A frozen waffle?" Gavin said.

"No, a message!" Sam handed Gavin a folded-up sheet of paper. "I thought of a way we can text each other even if we don't have phones. You'll need to get a notebook like the one I have. And you'll have to learn some secret codes."

Gavin unfolded the note. "Sam, this doesn't make any sense. It says *7-4-11-11-14 6-0-21-8-13. 19-7-8-18 8-18 0 12-4-*

*18-18-0-6-4 8-13 18-4-2-17-4-19 2-14-3-4
5-17-14-12 18-0-12."*

"It's in code!" Sam told him. "You can try to figure it out, or I can give you the code-buster book I wrote last night. Well, I copied and pasted it from the Internet and then printed out a copy for you. That's almost the same as writing it."

Sam reached into his backpack again and pulled out the book he'd made for Gavin. He'd printed out three different codes and sample messages on a sheet of paper and folded the paper in half long-wise so it looked like the world's longest, skinniest, shortest book.

"It's the first code on the sheet," Sam told Gavin, handing him the code-buster book.

"So if I see a zero, that means it's really

the letter *A*?" Gavin asked, reading the paper.

"Right," Sam said. "And if you see a twelve, that means it's an *M*. It's really easy once you get it."

"Cool!" Gavin said. He pulled a pencil out of his backpack's front pocket. "I'm going to get to work on it now!"

Gavin was still decoding the message when the school bus pulled up in front of the school five minutes later. Sam realized that it was a lot more fun to write a message in a secret code than to watch someone decode it. He also realized that until everyone had memorized the secret codes, they had better keep their messages short.

"So are we the only ones who are going to do this?" Gavin asked Sam as they

45

walked down the hallway to Mr. Pell's second-grade classroom. "Or are we going to get other people to do it too?"

"I thought maybe the members of our detective club might want to send messages," Sam said. "Like if we're working on a case and find clues we don't want anyone else to know about."

"That's a great idea!" Gavin said. "It will make our secret detective club even more secret. So where can we get notebooks like yours?"

"School store—fifty cents," Sam told him. "I'm going to get another one, so that I have a message notebook and an information notebook."

"You really *are* making your own phone," Gavin said, sounding impressed. He hung his backpack above his cubby outside of

Mr. Pell's classroom. "Now all you need to do is figure out how to call someone."

"I don't really like talking on the phone, so I don't mind not having that part," Sam said as he put his lunch in his cubby. "But I wish I had a camera. I'm going to ask my mom if I can use her old camera."

"Or you could just get another note-book," Gavin said, opening the door to their classroom.

Sam followed Gavin inside. "What do you mean?"

"You already have one notebook that's like the computer part of a phone, right? And next you're going to get a notebook you can send messages with." Gavin plopped down at his desk and turned to look at Sam. "So why not get another notebook to draw pictures of the things you see? Drawing a picture isn't as fast as taking a picture, but a picture is a picture, am I right?"

Sam guessed Gavin was right. Still, three notebooks was a lot of notebooks.

"If you made your message notebook and your camera notebook look like your information notebook, it would look like you had three phones," Gavin said. "I don't even know any grown-ups with three phones."

"I don't know any grown-ups with two phones," Sam said. "Most people just have one."

Sam sat down at his desk and checked the board. Checking the board was the first thing they were supposed to do every morning after they sat down in their seats so they would know their schedule for the day. Today they were doing math first, then they were going to Miss Fran's classroom to do art. Sam wondered if Miss Fran could teach him how to draw pictures that looked like real photographs.

Sam wouldn't mind using his mom's old camera if she'd let him, but the fact was, his mom's old camera wouldn't fit in his pocket. Another notebook would. Sam had four pockets in all, so if he wanted, he could have four notebooks. But what would he use his fourth notebook for?

Maybe nothing, he thought. Or maybe he could write a story in the fourth notebook. His mom could read books on her phone, and Sam thought it would be nice to be able to pull a notebook from his pocket and read a story whenever he wanted.

All of a sudden Sam had a lot of plans. Did he have too many plans?

Sam shook his head. There was no such thing as too many plans.

He was pretty sure he had exactly the right number.

Chapter Five

Showdown at the School Store

At lunchtime, Sam and Gavin decided to use their milk money to buy notebooks instead of milk, which is why they had to stop at a water fountain on the way to the school store.

"Too bad I had a peanut butter sandwich today," Gavin told Sam after he'd spent what seemed like a whole minute taking a drink. "By the time I was done eating, I thought my mouth was going to stay glued together forever."

"It was a good thing I had that apple," Sam said, leaning down to reach the fountain spout. "Having an apple is almost as good as having apple juice."

"If you chew it long enough, it's the exact same thing as having apple juice," Gavin said. "Except for the peel. Peels aren't very juicy."

There were three kids ahead of them in line when they got to the school store, which was really just a closet with the kind of door that had a top half and a bottom half. When the school store was open, the top half of the door was open, but the bottom was closed. When the store was closed, both halves of the door were closed.

"I can't wait until I'm in fifth grade and can work at the store," Gavin said to Sam as they waited in line.

"I don't know if I want to work in the store," Sam said. "Annabelle says it doesn't pay anything and all your friends will stop by and ask you for free stuff."

"I wouldn't do it for the money," Gavin said. "I'd do it because I really love how pencils smell."

When Sam reached the front of the line, the boy working behind the counter asked, "What do you want, peewee?"

"Not to be called a peewee," Sam said. "Especially since I'm tall for my age."

The boy laughed. "Okay, Mr. Tall Guy, what can I get you?"

Sam put two quarters on the counter, which was just a ledge attached by hinges to the lower half of the door. "I would like one notebook, please. The little kind of notebook that's held together at the top, not the side."

The boy reached behind him, pulled something out of a box, and slapped it on the counter. It was a small blue notebook, but the spiral wire holding the pages together was on the side, not on the top.

"That's not the right kind," Sam said. "I want the kind where you can flip the pages over the top, not over to the side. I know you have that kind, because I already have one I bought here last week."

"What's the difference?" the boy said. "Paper is paper."

"Sir!" Gavin said, stepping up so he was standing by Sam's side. "The customer is always right, sir!"

"You guys aren't customers, you're pipsqueaks." The boy looked over Sam's

and Gavin's heads. "Who's next?"

"We're next," Sam insisted. "We're right now."

"Sorry," the boy said. "You have to be at least as tall as my chin to get notebooks that have the top spiral. Too bad, so sad, goodbye."

Sam didn't know what to do. Peeking over the boy's shoulder, he could see a stack of little notebooks—*his* kind of little notebook—on a shelf. "All you have to do is get two of those notebooks on the shelf behind you," he said. "We don't even care what color."

"I'd like green, actually," Gavin said. "But red's okay too."

"Next!" the boy said, ignoring them.

The kids in line behind Sam and Gavin started to grumble. "Maybe we ought to come back another time," Gavin whispered to Sam. "I don't want to get in trouble."

"He's the one who should get in trouble," Sam whispered back. "He can't *not* sell us a notebook if we've got the money."

"Notebooks are now twenty dollars," the boy behind the counter announced. He looked at Sam. "Do you have twenty dollars?"

Now Sam was getting mad. Not only was this boy being a jerk, but once Sam and Gavin bought their notebooks, they were supposed to meet Emily, Rashid, and the other members of their detective club on the playground. Pretty soon it would be too late and they'd have to go back to their classroom.

Sam looked around. He wished some

big kid in line would come forward and make the boy behind the counter do the right thing. But everybody in line behind him looked annoyed, like they wished Sam and Gavin would just go away. Sam looked at the boy inside the store. He was acting like Sam and Gavin didn't even exist. Fine, Sam thought. He'd just have to take care of this himself then.

Sam's thoughts were braver than he was. "Give me your quarters," he said to Gavin in a shaky voice that matched his shaky knees. But when Gavin started to ask why, Sam's voice got a little stronger. "Just give me your quarters, okay?"

Gavin handed Sam two quarters. Sam took his own two quarters from the counter, so that he had four quarters in his hand. With his other hand, he grabbed the doorknob and pushed open the bottom half of the school store door. The boy in the store had to take a few steps back, which gave Sam room to step in.

"I'm putting these quarters on the shelf and taking two notebooks," Sam told the boy, whose face was turning a dangerous shade of red. "I'm getting a green one for Gavin and a blue one for me." He reached past the boy and took the notebooks.

"You're in big trouble, kid!" the boy yelled as Sam scooted back out into the hallway. "Big trouble!"

Now Sam's knees were wobbly instead of shaky, like they had turned into Jell-O. He'd never gotten in trouble at school before. He wondered if he'd get kicked out.

"Run, Sam!" Gavin yelled. "He'll never catch us!"

Sam and Gavin took off down the hall. There was a thumping noise in Sam's ears that made it hard to hear anything else. Was the boy about to catch them? He didn't want to turn around to look, but finally he did.

Nobody was there.

"He didn't chase us!" Sam called to Gavin, who was still running. "We're safe!"

Gavin thudded to a stop. "You mean he didn't even follow us?"

"Doesn't look like it," Sam said, panting. He handed Gavin his green notebook. "I hope he's not there tomorrow when I bring a dollar to buy two more notebooks."

"Two more notebooks?" Gavin looked confused. "I thought you were just going to have three notebooks."

"I decided I wanted a fourth notebook

to write stories in," Sam explained.

"Frozen-waffle stories?"

Sam nodded. "I thought I might write a story about how a frozen waffle got caught trying to sneak out of the freezer—"

"There they are!" The school-store boy stood at the other end of the hallway, pointing at Sam and Gavin. "They're the ones who stole the notebooks!"

Now Sam's entire body felt wobbly. Mr. Cameron, the school's vice principal, was standing next to the boy. "Are you sure, Jackson?"

"Positive! That's definitely them."

"Boys!" Mr. Cameron called down the hall. "Come here, please!"

Sam and Gavin looked at each other. Maybe they should just keep running, Sam thought, but where would they run to? Their houses were a ten-minute bus ride away.

"Right now, boys!" Mr. Cameron said. "We need to talk."

Sam's stomach started to hurt. He thought he might cry, and he hated to cry at school. So far this year he'd only cried once, when Will had kicked a soc-cer ball all the way down the field, and the ball had hit Sam in the back by accident. Hard. No one could have blamed Sam for crying, espe-cially when Will started to cry too.

62

"Come on, Sam," Gavin whispered, grabbing Sam's arm. "We didn't do anything wrong. Let's go tell Mr. Cameron what happened—how that boy wouldn't sell us the notebooks we wanted."

Sam followed Gavin down the hallway, his feet moving a lot slower than usual. But even though he was going as slow as he could, they finally reached Mr. Cameron and the school-store boy.

"So Jackson says you boys stole two notebooks from the store," Mr. Cameron said. He sounded more interested than mad. "Do you want to tell me what happened?"

"That one pushed open the door," Jackson said, pointing at Sam. "He grabbed two notebooks and ran out. That's the whole story."

"No, it's not!" Gavin said. "He paid for the notebooks, for one thing."

Jackson shoved his hands in his pockets and shrugged. "I didn't see any money."

"And for another thing," Sam said, finally finding his voice, "you ignored me when I asked for the kind of notebooks we wanted." He pulled the blue notebook from his pocket and showed it to Mr. Cameron. "We wanted this kind, but he tried to make us buy the other kind."

"See! Stolen merchandise, right there!" Jackson yelled. "Caught red-handed."

"I didn't steal anything," Sam said. "I bet you have the four quarters I put on the shelf right there in your pocket."

Mr. Cameron turned to Jackson. "Do you have the quarters in your pocket, Jackson?"

"I have four of *my* quarters in my pocket," Jackson said. "That's not against the law, is it?"

Mr. Cameron looked at Sam and Gavin. "I'm going to ask the children who were in the line behind you what happened. You boys are in Mr. Pell's class, correct?"

Sam and Gavin nodded their heads. "Very well then," Mr. Cameron continued. "If the other children support your story, I will consider this matter closed—though in the future, I'd ask you to come to me when you have a problem. If the children tell me that Jackson's story is correct, then I'll send a note to Mr. Pell's classroom asking you to come see me in my office."

"Could you send a note either way?" Sam asked. "Otherwise I'll spend the rest of my life feeling nervous about it."

"Fair enough," Mr. Cameron said. "Jackson, I'll close up the store. You go back to your classroom. Lunchtime is almost over."

Jackson waited until Mr. Cameron was all the way down the hall, and then he turned to Sam and Gavin. "You better hope those other kids say my side of the story is right. Because if I get in trouble over this, you're going to get in even more trouble."

"That doesn't make sense," Gavin said. "If you get in trouble, then that means we're not in trouble at all."

"You'll be in trouble with *me*," Jackson

said. "Believe me, that's worse than being in trouble with Mr. Cameron."

With that, Jackson turned and walked toward the fifth-grade hall. Sam and Gavin looked at each other. Gavin was pale. Sam could feel his stomach *really* hurting now.

"I'm starting to wish I'd stayed home today," Gavin told Sam.

Sam nodded. "I kind of wish we'd waited until tomorrow to buy our notebooks."

"At least we didn't have to give the notebooks back," Gavin said as he and Sam started walking toward Mr. Pell's room. "And if everybody tells Mr. Cameron the truth about what happened, then Jackson will probably get fired and we can buy more notebooks tomorrow. I'd really like to read the frozen-waffle story you're planning to write."

Sam would really like to *write* the frozen-waffle story. But mostly what he wanted was for Jackson not to beat him up.

Sam had the feeling it was going to be a very long afternoon.

Chapter Six

Nothing But Trouble

That night Sam sat his desk and tried to draw a picture of Jackson, the school-store boy. In art class, Miss Fran had told Sam that he could learn how to draw pictures that looked like photographs, but he could also draw pictures that didn't look like photographs and they still would be good pictures. Right now Sam really wanted the picture to look real. That way if Jackson punched him in the mouth and

Sam couldn't talk, he could show it to people so that they would know who to put in jail.

"Do you think we should tell someone that Jackson says he's going to beat us up?" Gavin had asked on the bus that afternoon. "That's what grown-ups always say you should do if someone's being a bully."

Sam had thought about it. "He didn't actually say he would beat us up. He just said we'd be in trouble if he got in trouble."

"I think he got in trouble," Gavin pointed out. "Since the note Mr. Cameron sent Mr. Pell said we weren't in trouble. Which means now we're in trouble."

"But not that we're going to get beat up," Sam argued. "He'll probably just say mean things about us. So what?"

Gavin shook his head. "I think it means he's going to punch us in the mouth. In both our mouths."

"Why would he punch us in the mouth?" Sam asked. "Why not the nose?"

"Because if he punches us in the mouth, our teeth will fall out and we won't be able to tell anyone who punched us."

Sam didn't really think Jackson was going to punch him in the mouth and make his teeth fall out. But he was drawing Jackson's picture just in case. What color eyes did he have? Sam couldn't remember. Maybe if he just drew really mean eyes, people would know who Sam meant.

Leaning back in his desk chair, Sam wondered if Gavin was right. Maybe they should tell a grown-up what Jackson had said. Sam had thought about telling Mr. Stockfish that afternoon, but Mrs. Kerner had been in the backyard when they got to her house, and she and Mr. Stockfish started talking about the movie they were going to see on Friday night, and then they argued about what was better—steak and baked potatoes or roast beef and mashed potatoes. It wasn't the sort of conversation where you could say, "I like mashed potatoes, and I think this boy at school might beat me up."

Sam thought about telling his parents, but what if they got mad because he took the notebooks from the store the wrong way? They might say Sam couldn't buy any more notebooks, and that would ruin his plans.

No, Sam decided he wouldn't say anything to any grown-ups. Probably everything would be okay. Besides, he still had a bunch of baby teeth, so it wouldn't matter if a few of them fell out when Jackson punched him.

Sam decided he'd rather think about buying two more notebooks than losing his teeth, so he pulled open his desk drawer and stuck his hand inside. He knew he had some tooth fairy quarters in there somewhere. His mom said he should keep his money in a piggy bank or at least in a plastic bag, but Sam liked to be surprised by his money. It was fun to look for a pencil and find a dollar bill rolled up beside it in his pencil box, and it was fun to feel around in the drawer for coins. Every kind of coin felt different.

Nickels and pennies had smooth edges, and quarters and dimes had rough edges. Quarters were a lot thicker than dimes, but they were almost the same size as nickels. It would be easy to mix up quarters and nickels if their edges were the same.

It didn't take Sam very long to find seven quarters, a poker chip, and a button. Seven quarters was a lot of quarters. If he wanted, Sam could buy three notebooks and still have one quarter left over. But if Sam bought three notebooks, he would have five notebooks in all, and he thought that might be too many notebooks. Probably one notebook for each pocket was enough. So tomorrow he would buy two more notebooks for a total of four.

Sam went downstairs to see if his dad would let him look through some more computer magazines for phone pictures. He didn't think people would really believe he had four phones, but it would be fun to pretend.

Sam's dad was sitting at the table in the storage room, working on his computer. "Hey, Sam the Man," he said when Sam walked in the room. "How was your day today?"

"You already asked me that at dinner," Sam said. "Everything's still the same, except I just found seven quarters."

"That's a lot of quarters," Sam's dad said. "What are you going to do with them?"

"I'm going to use four of them to buy notebooks," Sam said.

"For your phone plan?"

Sam nodded. "Then I'll have an information notebook, a message notebook, a camera notebook, and a story notebook. It will almost be as good as having a real phone."

"I think it will be even better," Sam's dad said. "So you're sure your day was okay?"

Sam looked at his dad. Why was he

so worried about what kind of day Sam had? "It was fun, except that I got sort of thirsty at lunch because I used my milk money to buy notebook number two—the one for messages."

"So you bought the notebook at the school store?" Sam's dad turned his chair all the way around so he was facing Sam directly. "And that went okay?"

Sam wondered if Mr. Cameron had called or e-mailed his dad about what happened. Maybe he should go ahead and say something about Jackson. But what could his dad do? Come with Sam to school and be his bodyguard?

Come to think of it, that wasn't a bad idea. Having a bodyguard would solve all of Sam's problems. But where could he find one?

"Everything went fine," Sam told his dad, feeling okay for the first time since lunch. A plan started to come together in his brain, and that always made Sam feel better. He wasn't sure if his plan would work, but it might work, and even if it didn't work, maybe it would lead him to an even better plan.

Instead of cutting out phone pictures for his notebooks, Sam went upstairs to talk to Annabelle.

"Janie Kramer," Annabelle told him the second Sam asked her for bodyguard recommendation. "She's small for her age, but super strong—and really tough. Last year, when she was a fourth grader, we let her play on the fifth-grade soccer team because she was fearless."

"I don't know," Sam said. "Would anyone really be afraid of a girl bodyguard?"

"Believe me, Sam the Man, people respect Janie," Annabelle said. "If she's your bodyguard, this Jackson kid will leave you alone."

That's all Sam wanted. Plus, he'd like to keep all of his teeth.

Annabelle opened her drawing pad to a blank sheet of paper and wrote something down. "Here," she said, ripping out the sheet and handing it to Sam. "Just give this to Janie in the morning, and I bet she'll help you out."

Sam took the paper to his room. Annabelle had written, *Please help my little brother and I'll help you out when you get to middle school. He needs you to look out for him for a few days and make sure a fifth grader named Jackson doesn't hit him or his friend Gavin. Signed, Annabelle Graham.*

Sam wished Annabelle still went to his school. She'd be a great bodyguard. But for now he'd have to keep his fingers crossed that Janie Kramer was up for the job.

Chapter Seven

The Bodyguard Plan

As soon as Sam walked through the school's front door the next morning, a girl wearing overalls and a baseball cap came up to him and tapped him on the shoulder. "Are you Sam Graham?" she asked.

"How did you know?" Sam asked.

"I'm Janie Kramer and it's my job to know," the girl said. "Plus, your sister texted my sister your picture."

"Why didn't she text you the picture?" Gavin, who was standing next to Sam, asked.

Janie Kramer held up her hands so Sam and Gavin could see they were empty. "No phone, dude. My parents are strict about screens. Suzzie—my sister?—she's in seventh grade, so she's got one. She and Annabelle know each other from swim team. So I hear you have a note for me?"

Sam dug into his backpack for Annabelle's note and handed it to Janie. Janie read it, nodded, and slipped it into her back pocket. "Okay, Sam Graham, here's the deal," she said. "I'm a busy person, but your sister's a friend, so I'm going to help you and your buddy out. I'll meet you guys here first thing every morning for the next week and walk you to your classroom, and

I'll wait with you in the bus line in the afternoon. I play soccer on the big field during morning and lunchtime recess, and you can come hang out with my team if you want. Nobody will bother you when you're with the Barracudas."

"Is that the name of your team?" Sam asked, imagining a pool full of sharp-toothed fish pushing a soccer ball around.

"You got it," Janie said. "And we don't put up with bullies like Jackson Grubb."

"How do you know that Jackson Grubb is the Jackson who's going to beat us up?" Gavin asked Janie as the three of them started down the hallway. "There are a lot of Jacksons in this school."

"Was it the school-store Jackson?" Janie asked, and when Sam and Gavin nodded, she said, "That's Jackson Grubb. So what room are you in?"

As they walked down the hall, Sam looked around for Jackson. Was he following them? Hiding around the next corner? Sam felt safer with Janie walking next to him, but he still couldn't help feeling nervous, like he was watching a scary movie where a monster could jump out in front of him at any second.

"I almost forgot!" Gavin said as they turned down the second-grade hallway. He pulled his notebook from his back pocket and held it out for Sam to see. "Look what I did, Sam!"

Gavin's notebook had a phone picture

on it, just like Sam's. "This is my texting notebook," he said. "I wrote a message for you in it—in secret code!"

"What in the bananas are you talking about?" Janie asked. "Let me see that!"

Gavin handed her the notebook. "It looks like a real phone, doesn't it? It was Sam's idea."

"That's pretty cool," Janie said. "I really thought it *was* a phone at first. So you're sending each other messages in code?"

Gavin nodded. "It was Sam's idea. Once our other friends get notebooks, we're all going to learn the same code. It'll be as good as texting."

"Especially if you don't have a real phone to text with," Janie agreed. "You little dudes have come up with a really neat idea."

Sam didn't know how he felt about being called a little dude. It was better than being called a pipsqueak or a pee-wee, he guessed, but not as good as being called "dude" or just plain Sam.

After Sam and Gavin sat down in their seats and read the daily schedule on the whiteboard, Sam opened up Gavin's notebook. On top of the first page, Gavin had written, *"18-14-2-10 12-14-13-10-4-24-18 0-17-4 19-7-4 1-4-18-19 12-14-13-10-4-24-18."*

"Guess what it says?" Gavin said.

"I'm not going to guess," Sam told him. "I'm going to figure out the code. That's the whole point."

First, Sam noticed that the two lon-gest words in Gavin's message were the same—*12-14-13-10-4-24-18*—so he decided to work on that word first. If Gavin was using the same code Sam had used in his message, then $0 = A$. Sam counted on his fingers until he got to twelve—otherwise known as the letter M. Two letters after M was O, so $14 = O$, which meant $13 = N$. M-O-N-

Sam didn't even have to figure out the code to know what this word was. Gavin loved sock monkeys, so the word had to be "monkeys". And—yep—$18 = S$. Sock Monkeys. Count on Gavin to write a message about sock monkeys, Sam thought.

He didn't have time to finish decoding Gavin's message before reading period started. That was okay, though. Sam had the feeling that a sock monkey message could wait.

As they were breaking into their

reading groups, Emily Early came over to Sam and said, "I bought two note-books at the school store this morning," she told him. "One for messages and one for bird names. Marja, Rashid, and Will bought notebooks too. Let's meet at recess to discuss our plans."

Sam nodded. "Tell everyone to come to the big field as soon as the bell rings."

"Why the big field?" Emily asked. "We usually meet next to the little field."

"I'll explain at recess," Sam told her.

"Okay," Emily said. "I'll bring the bin-oculars so we can look at birds after we're done talking."

Sam liked that idea. If they had binoc-ulars, they could also look out for Jackson Grubb. Sam wondered what a Jackson Grubb bird would look like. Maybe a vulture. Sam had seen a vulture once when he and his dad were driving to the store. It had been so ugly that Sam had to close his eyes.

Sam hoped there would be time at lunch to buy a notebook so he could use it as a camera and draw a picture of Jackson the Vulture Bird in it.

He hoped that Jackson the Vulture Bird wouldn't swoop down and get him.

Sam thought maybe it was time to stop thinking about about Jackson Grubb, the person *and* the bird. It wasn't good to have so many nervous-making thoughts first thing in the morning.

At recess, the members of the World's Greatest Detective and Bird-watching Club met at the big field where the fourth and fifth graders played soccer. Janie Kramer waved at Sam when she saw him. "Everything okay, little dude?" she called.

Sam waved back. "Everything's fine," he called.

"Why did she ask you that?" Marja wanted to know. "What does she think might be wrong?"

"Jackson Grubb is going to beat us up," Gavin told her. "Janie's our bodyguard."

"I think I'd be a pretty good bodyguard," Marja said. "I'm not afraid to bite people."

"Me either," Gavin said. "Except some people taste funny. My sister tastes like salt."

"I'm pretty sure everybody tastes like salt," Rashid told him. "Because of sweat."

"She also tastes like peanut butter,"

90

Gavin said. "The smooth kind."

"Could we maybe talk about something else?" Emily asked. "Like what kind of messages we should send one another? I think we should only send messages that are important."

"Like, 'Here comes Jackson and he looks really mad so you better hide!'" Gavin said. "That would be really important."

"Or 'I saw a kid with Mr. Pell's stolen wallet,'" Will said. "Something that has to do with our detective club work."

"Mr. Pell's wallet got stolen?" Marja asked.

"No, that's just an example," Will told her. "Who would steal Mr. Pell's wallet?"

"Somebody might," Marja said. "Maybe we should be bodyguards for Mr. Pell."

"Maybe we should look at birds now," Sam said. "When we go back inside, I'll give everybody the secret code sheet I printed out. The code is pretty easy, once you understand it."

Morning recess didn't last very long, and soon the recess duty teachers were blowing their whistles for everybody to go in. On the way to his classroom, Sam stopped at his cubby so he could get the code sheets to pass out to everyone. He unzipped his backpack and pulled out a folder. Putting the sheets in a folder had made Sam feel very professional and grown-up. But now he saw someone had drawn a picture on the folder, a picture that hadn't been there this morning. It was a giant eye, and underneath it were the words

WHEN NOBODY'S LOOKING, I'LL BE WAITING.

Sam turned around fast, expecting to see Jackson Grubb standing behind him. It had to be Jackson who wrote on his folder, right? Feeling a little shaky, he leaned back against the cubby wall. What was Jackson going to do to him exactly? Sam wasn't sure what the message meant, to be honest. Waiting for what? Why wait? Why not do

WHEN NOBODY'S LOOKING I'LL BE WAITING!

something? When Sam was at home and nobody was looking, sometimes he liked to grab a couple cookies from the cookie jar, even though he was only supposed to eat cookies after dinner. Sometimes when nobody was looking, Sam picked his nose. But he never just stood around and waited because no one was looking.

Sam decided to take the code sheets out of the folder and put the folder back into his backpack. If he showed everybody the folder right now, they'd make a big deal out of it, and then Mr. Pell would say, "What's going on here?" and then Jackson Grubb would get in even more trouble and Sam would get punched even harder.

Because Sam might not know what the message meant, but he was pretty sure Jackson Grubb was the one who wrote it.

Chapter Eight

Balloon Problems

Mr. Stockfish was examining a red leaf with a little black bump on it. "When I was a kid I was taught that these bumps were bug eggs," he told Sam. "But recently I found out that they could also just be spots where bugs have taken a bite out of the leaves."

"How can you tell the difference?" Sam asked.

"I don't know," Mr. Stockfish said. "I've

looked it up, but I can't find information that says for sure."

"Not even on your phone?"

"Not even on my phone," Mr. Stockfish said, rolling his eyes. "Imagine that."

The afternoon was windy and leaves were blowing off the trees all around them. Sam wondered if any of his neighbors would pay him to rake the leaves from their yards. He wondered if he should start a leaf collection. Maybe he would only collect leaves with bug bumps on them. He could set up a museum in the garage, so everyone could come see his buggy leaves.

Sam liked that plan. For one thing, it didn't make his stomach hurt. He was tired of thinking about things that made his stomach hurt. Riding home

from school on the bus, Sam couldn't stop thinking about Jackson Grubb's face staring at him from the hallway outside of Mr. Pell's classroom that afternoon before the last bell rang. Sam had been copying down spelling words from the board when Gavin had turned around and poked him in the shoulder with his pencil.

"He's out there, Sam!" Gavin had whispered, and sure enough, Jackson was looking in through the classroom door's long, skinny window. Sam could only see half of his face, but even half of Jackson Grubb's face was enough to make him wish he were home and hiding in his bedroom closet.

"What would you do if someone was after you?" he asked Mr. Stockfish now, leaning down to pluck a leaf off the sidewalk. Sam tried to sound like he didn't really care, that he was just trying to make conversation.

"What kind of someone?" Mr. Stockfish stopped walking and turned to look at Sam. "Like someone who was mad at me?"

Sam nodded, examining his leaf so he wouldn't have to look Mr. Stockfish in the eye.

"Well, why is this person mad at me?" Mr. Stockfish asked. "Is it a misunderstanding? Did I take something from him? Did I say something mean about him behind his back?"

Sam and Mr. Stockfish began walking again. They were close enough to Mrs. Kerner's house that Sam thought he could hear the chickens clucking in the backyard. "Maybe this person is mad because you got him in trouble," Sam said. "Except you didn't, not really. He got himself in trouble."

"But he blames you," Mr. Stockfish concluded. "What's going on, Sam?"

"Nothing," Sam said. "I was just thinking."

"Hmmm," Mr. Stockfish said in a grumbly sort of voice. "You were just thinking about someone being mad at you for something you didn't do."

"Well, I sort of did do something," Sam said.

"You did?"

Sam realized he'd said something he hadn't meant to say. "Not me. I wasn't talking about me. Could we stop talking now?"

They'd reached the gate to Mrs. Kerner's backyard. Sam opened it and let Mr. Stockfish through, and then followed him to the chicken coop. When the chickens saw Sam and Mr. Stockfish, they clucked and clacked, which Sam thought was their way of saying hello.

Sam went to the metal trash can that Mrs. Kerner kept the chicken feed in and lifted up the lid. He dipped in the big plastic scoop and filled it up, and then he took it over to the coop to fill the chicken's feeder. All eight chickens gathered around his ankles, making their different chicken noises—not just clucks and clacks, but also squawks and peeps. The noises were friendly, like the chickens were happy to see Sam and not just because he was feeding them.

Sam checked the waterer, which was full, and then looked at the chicken litter, which was the straw and hay that covered the floor of the coop. It was Sam's job to change the litter every month or whenever it started to get icky. The straw and hay still looked pretty clean to Sam, so he could probably wait another week to change it out.

By the time Sam sat down in the lawn chair next to Mr. Stockfish, he felt a lot better. He decided to take out his camera notebook and draw a picture of the chicken coop.

"How many notebooks do you have

now?" Mr. Stockfish wanted to know. "It seems like a lot."

"I bought two new notebooks today, so I have four," Sam told him. "Except I'm trying to remember to call them 'phones' and not 'notebooks.'"

"I'll try to remember too," Mr. Stockfish promised, and then he leaned back and closed his eyes. "Let me know when Leroy is done eating."

Sam started to draw. He thought about walking to the school store with Gavin that afternoon. Nothing had happened, but Sam had been worried that something *would* happen, which was almost as bad as something happening. Once he and Gavin had bought their notebooks and walked outside to the big field, Sam had relaxed. But then later on Jackson's face had appeared in the classroom door window, and Sam had gotten all nervous again.

He didn't feel nervous now, Sam realized. Drawing made him feel relaxed. So did taking care of the chickens. So did sitting next to Mr. Stockfish, now that Sam thought about it. Mr. Stockfish was cranky, but Sam knew if he asked, Mr. Stockfish would help him. But he would also probably say something to Sam's parents, who were already worried—at least his dad *seemed* a little worried. Then Sam's parents would call Mr. Cameron, who would probably call Jackson Grubb's parents, and Jackson Grubb would get in more trouble.

And the more trouble Jackson got in, the more trouble Sam would be in with

Jackson Grubb. Any way that Sam tried to think about it, he always came back to Jackson Grubb's face in the window for the rest of Sam's life.

Sam liked drawing the chicken wire that made the chicken coop's walls. Mr. Stockfish said the shapes the wire made were called hexagons. They had six sides, and there were hundreds of them, it seemed like to Sam. He decided to draw exactly a hundred, and worked hard at making each hexagon even, like his picture really was a photograph.

After a couple tries, Sam finally figured out how small he needed to draw the wire hexagons in order to fit a hundred on a notebook page. He was up to number thirty-two when he glanced up and saw that the chickens were done eating and were now wandering around the coop.

"Leroy's finished with his lunch," Sam told Mr. Stockfish, who let out a big snore and then shuddered before opening his eyes.

"What was that, Sam?" he asked. "It's time to get up?"

"It's not morning, it's afternoon," Sam said. "And Leroy is done eating."

Mr. Stockfish pushed himself up in his chair. "Go grab her for me, would you?"

Sam put his notebook back in his pocket and went to get Leroy. When he came back, he carefully placed the chicken in Mr. Stockfish's lap. Mr. Stockfish patted the top of Leroy's head and closed his eyes again.

"Thank you, Sam," he said.

"You're welcome," Sam replied, sitting

back down. "Do you want me to wake you up if you fall back asleep?"

"I'm not sleeping," Mr. Stockfish said. "I'm meditating. It relaxes me."

After a few more minutes of meditating, Mr. Stockfish opened his eyes. "The problem with not doing anything about your problems is that they get bigger, not smaller. And you know where they get biggest of all?"

Sam shook his head. He wasn't sure he understood Mr. Stockfish's question.

"They get biggest of all in your head, Sam the Man," Mr. Stockfish said. "They're like balloons that just keep filling up with air until they take up all the space in your brain."

"So what do you do to keep them from filling all the way up?" Sam asked.

Mr. Stockfish scratched Leroy behind her ears. "You've got to pop them before they get too big."

"I don't like popping balloons," Sam said.

"Neither do I," Mr. Stockfish said. "But I'd rather pop a balloon than wait around for someone else to pop it."

Sam couldn't disagree with that. Even if a person with a balloon was standing right in front of him saying, "I'm going to pop this balloon on the count of three—one-two-three!", Sam still jumped.

Just as Sam was going to ask Mr. Stockfish more about the balloon that Sam needed to pop, Mrs. Kerner walked out onto her deck and called, "Yoo-hoo! Who needs a snack?"

"I could use some pretzels and some lemonade," Mr. Stockfish said, gently putting Leroy on the ground and pushing himself out of his chair. "How about you, Sam?"

"Okay," Sam said. Maybe a snack would help him think better. Because Sam wasn't sure what the balloon in his head was. Was Jackson Grubb the balloon that was getting bigger and bigger? Was getting punched in the mouth the balloon in Sam's head?

Or maybe being afraid of Jackson for the rest of his life was Sam's balloon.

Yes, Sam was pretty sure that being afraid was his balloon.

He just wished he knew how to pop it.

Chapter Nine

The Balloon-Pop Plan

Now that Sam had a story notebook, he was ready to write his waffle story, but he couldn't remember if frozen waffles used to be called "froffles" or "fraffles." He knew he'd written it down, so at dinner that night he took out his information notebook to look up the facts that he needed.

"No phones at the table, Sam," his mom said when Sam put his notebook next to his plate.

"Eyes on each other, not on screens, Sam the Man," his dad added.

Sam stared at his parents. "Do you mean that?" he asked. "You know this isn't a real phone, right?"

"What *is* a phone?" his dad asked as he poked at a meatball with his fork, a thoughtful expression on his face. "Is it not a device for communication?"

Sam shrugged. He guessed so.

"And in this day and age, is a phone not also a computer?" Sam's dad continued, and Sam nodded.

"And is a computer not a device for storing and processing data?" Sam's dad asked, and when Sam nodded again, he said, "So why can't we call your notebook a phone?"

Sam's dad leaned back in his chair, looking pleased with himself.

"Is this just another way of telling Sam to put his notebook back in his pocket?" Annabelle asked as she reached for the bread basket.

"Sort of," Sam's dad said. "But I also think I'm right."

"I think you're *sort of* right," Sam's mom said. "Phones and computers also send out information using wires or electromagnetic systems. Sam's notebook can't do that."

"I don't need wires," Sam told his mom. "I can just pass my phone to somebody else using my hand."

"There you have it!" Sam's dad said. "That means that your notebook really is a phone and it's time to put your phone away."

Sam slipped his notebook back into

his pocket. He guessed he would have to think about his story after dinner. He already knew some things about it. The hero of his story was named Frozen Fred. Frozen Fred wanted to go to the monster truck show downtown, but he knew if he left the freezer, pretty soon he wouldn't be frozen anymore. So how could he go to the monster truck show without thawing out?

"What's the best way to stay cold for a long time?" Sam asked his family as he twirled some strands of spaghetti onto his fork. "Maybe cover yourself up with snow?"

"Sure, if there's snow on the ground outside," Sam's dad said. "But if it was summer, you could put ice packs under your clothes."

"Waffles don't wear clothes," Sam said. "So I guess I mean what's the best way for a waffle to stay frozen if it gets out of the freezer?"

"If it hopped from a freezer into a cooler, it would stay frozen for a little while," Annabelle said. "Especially if the cooler was filled with ice."

"Exactly what are you planning, Sam the Man?" Sam's mom asked, sounding suspicious.

Sam wriggled his eyebrows, trying to look mysterious. "It's a secret," he told her. "May I please be excused?"

"As long as you promise to stay out of the freezer," Sam's mom said.

Sam went upstairs to his room and sat at his desk. He took a pencil out of his top drawer and pulled his story notebook out of his pocket. *The Great Frozen Waffle Escape*, he wrote at the top of the first page. And then he wrote,

One day Fred the Frozen Waffle wanted to go to the monster truck show. There was only one problem. What if he got too warm? Would he get unfroze?

Sam stopped writing. Was "unfroze" a word? He remembered one of Mr. Pell's rules about writing: Worry about spelling later. Sam would worry about words later too.

Frozen Fred had a problem. If he got unfroze, he wouldn't be Frozen Fred anymore. If he was Unfroze Fred, he wouldn't be able to roll around like a wheel.

So what could Frozen Fred do? He asked his friend Frozen Peas, "How do I stay froze when I leave the freezer?"

"*If I could fly, you could ride on my back and stay cold,*" Frozen Peas said. "*But I can't move at all. I wish I was more like you.*"

Poor Frozen Peas, Sam thought. He was stuck inside the freezer forever, or at least until someone wanted peas for dinner. Sam guessed that Frozen Fred was stuck, too, unless he knew how to open the freezer door. That was another problem that needed to be solved.

Sam wondered if all of Frozen Fred's problems would blow up like balloons and suddenly pop? Not if someone opened the freezer door! Sam started writing again. *Just then the door opened. Fred rolled out onto the kitchen*

115

floor and to the door. "Somebody catch that waffle!" a man's voice yelled. Fred kept rolling.

That's one balloon that got popped, Sam thought. It was fun popping balloon problems, at least when they weren't *your* balloon problems. Other people's problems were always easier, especially if those other people were waffles.

Or, Sam thought, if those other people were Gavin.

When Jackson Grubbs had shown up in Mr. Pell's window that afternoon, he wasn't just shooting mean looks at Sam, he was shooting them at Gavin, too. Maybe Sam should think about solving Gavin's problem instead of solving Sam's problem.

Sam felt a lot braver when he thought

about helping his friend instead of worrying about himself.

Okay then, Sam thought, standing up. What was Gavin's problem? What was his balloon? Was it that Jackson might punch him in the mouth and make his teeth fall out?

No, Sam thought. Gavin's problem was the same as Sam's. Gavin's problem was that he had to walk around being afraid all the time.

So how could Sam help Gavin stop being afraid?

How could he pop the balloon of afraidness?

He could punch Jackson Grubb in the mouth and make *him* afraid all the time, Sam thought. He sort of liked that idea, except for the fact that Jackson Grubb was a lot bigger than him. And also, Sam didn't want to make somebody afraid all the time. It seemed mean to him, and also exhausting.

So maybe Sam and Gavin could do something that would make Jackson Grubb exhausted. Maybe instead of being afraid of Jackson following them around all the time, maybe they could follow Jackson around all the time.

They should probably take their body-guard with them, Sam thought, just in case it took Jackson a while to get tired of being mean.

Sam went back to his desk and took out his message notebook. He would write a message to Gavin about his new plan and give it to him first thing in the morning. *3-4-0-17 6-0-21-8-13*, he began, and then he stopped. He'd had a lot of good plans lately, but he was starting to wonder if writing all his messages in code was one of them. Maybe sometimes writing in code was a good idea, Sam decided. But other times writing fast was better.

Dear Gavin, he started again. *From now on, wherever Jackson Grubb goes, we go too. Deal? Signed, Sam Graham.*

Sam closed his notebook and smiled. It felt good to help a friend out.

Chapter Ten

The Annoying Pipsqueaks Strike Again

Janie Kramer was waiting for Sam and Gavin at the school entrance the next morning. When she saw them, she held up a little notebook, the kind with the wire on top.

"This phone thing is taking off," she said. "I told my friends about what you were doing, and they totally loved the idea. I think we bought all the notebooks in the school store."

"How many notebooks do you have?" Sam asked as they started walking down the hallway. "I've got four."

"Four?" Janie's eyes grew wide. "Holy moly! Where do you keep them all?"

"I've got four pockets in my pants," Sam told her. "I keep a notebook in each one. The front ones sort of hurt when I sit down, but that's okay."

"They also get bent up," Gavin pointed out. "I noticed that about your message notebook." He turned to Sam. "Should we tell her about our new plan?"

"You've got a plan?" Janie asked. "Lay it on me, little brother."

Sam liked the idea of being Janie's little brother, at least at school. In his experience, big sisters did a good job of helping little brothers out, and Sam could use all the help he could get.

"Do you know where Jackson Grubb is right now?" he asked Janie. "Because we want to go stare at him."

"You want to stare at Jackson?" Janie gave Sam a funny look. "I thought you were trying to avoid him."

"We were," Sam said. "But we decided to pop the balloon instead."

"You realize that nothing you're saying makes any sense right now," Janie said. "But what the hey, you're a kid with good ideas. Let's go."

So instead of walking to the second-grade hallway, Sam, Gavin, and Janie went over to the fourth- and fifth-grade hallway. "Jackson's in Mrs. Hu's homeroom," Janie said. "I saw him earlier in the hallway, so he's probably inside already."

The door to Mrs. Hu's classroom was open. Sure enough, there was Jackson Grubb over by the window, talking to two other boys.

Sam turned to Gavin. "Are you ready to stare?"

"Ready, Eddie," Gavin said, coming over so he and Sam were standing side by side. "Should we make mean faces too?"

"I think staring is good enough," Sam said.

It took a minute before anyone noticed Sam and Gavin standing at the classroom door. Once one person noticed, everybody noticed, including Jackson Grubb.

"What are you pipsqueaks doing here?" he called from across the classroom. "Why aren't you over in Babyville?"

"Don't say anything," Sam whispered

to Gavin. "Just let him talk."

"Why are those kids staring at you?" another kid in the classroom asked Jackson. "Do you owe them money?"

"They're idiots," Jackson said. "Just ignore them."

"The bell's about to ring," Janie said from behind Sam and Gavin. "You guys better head to your classroom."

Sam nodded. "Okay," he said. He turned back to Jackson. "See you at recess," he called.

"I thought we weren't going to say anything," Gavin said as he and Sam headed for Mr. Pell's room. "So why'd you say anything?"

"Because it's Jackson's turn to worry for a change," Sam said. "We might not be as big as fifth graders, and we might not

be as fast as fifth graders, but we can be as annoying as fifth graders."

"So you think Jackson's going to be worried about us annoying him all day?"

Sam shrugged. "He might be. And when he gets tired of being annoyed, he'll leave us alone."

"Maybe," Gavin said as they reached their classroom. "Or maybe he'll just want to punch us even more."

The bell rang before Sam had a chance to worry about that. He hurried inside to his desk, where he found four little notebooks waiting for him.

"Text messages!" Gavin said. "What do they say?"

"I don't know yet," Sam said. "I'll read them later."

Sam put the four notebooks in a pile

and set the pile on the top left-hand corner of his desk. He really wanted to read the messages now, but the rule was that you had to look at the whiteboard as soon as you sat down. Sam checked the schedule and saw they were doing science first, so he pulled out his science notebook and his pencil from the front of his desk. Mr. Pell liked his students to be ready to learn.

Sam's favorite part of science was when they did projects, especially projects where they went outside, like when they were studying clouds. Sam also liked it when Mr. Pell set up tables in the back of the classroom to do experiments. A few weeks ago they had made batteries out of lemons, which had been fun until a few people started squirting lemon juice at one another.

Today, though, they were doing the most boring science thing in the world: science vocabulary. Every time they started a new unit, Mr. Pell made them learn new scientific terms. He read out a vocabulary list and everyone had to write down the words and what they thought the words meant. Sam thought this would be okay if you could write funny things down when you didn't know the answers, but Mr. Pell wanted you to be serious and make good guesses when you didn't know for sure what a word meant.

"Okay, today's first word is *energy*," Mr. Pell told them. "So write down your definition for energy."

Energy. That was easy, Sam thought. Energy was . . . was . . . what was it? Sam felt like he knew what energy was, but he didn't know how to say it. He decided to write down *Energy is what makes things move*, even though he wasn't sure if that was exactly right.

The next word was motion. Sam wrote *Motion is things moving*, which he also thought was sort of right if not exactly right. But he had no idea what to write down for the third word. *Vibrations*? He'd heard the word before, but he didn't know what it meant at all.

It was almost like Mr. Pell had read Sam's mind. "Remember, even if you don't know the definition, you can still guess. You can even draw a picture."

Sam didn't know how he could draw a picture of something when he had no idea what it was. He'd rather draw a picture of a chicken coop. Speaking of which . . .

Sam pulled his camera notebook out of his back pocket so he could see what he'd drawn the day before. His chicken coop picture still needed a lot of hexagons, Sam thought, but it was going to look super cool when he—

Mr. Pell was suddenly standing next to Sam's desk. "Sam? What are you doing?"

"I'm—I'm just—uh . . ."

Gavin turned around. "Sam's looking at his camera," he explained to Mr. Pell in a helpful tone of voice. "Maybe he's got a picture of a vibration in there."

"His camera?" Mr. Pell looked at Sam. "Are you hiding a phone in your desk, Sam?"

Sam held up his camera notebook to Mr. Pell. "He means my notebook. I use it like a camera."

"Okay, well, why don't you let me keep your camera for you for the rest of the morning," Mr. Pell said, and a bunch of people giggled. Mr. Pell pointed to the pile of notebooks on the corner of Sam's desk. "Are those cameras too?"

"Those are texts," Sam explained. "I'm not sure who they're from. Probably Emily and Will."

"And me," Marja said. "I sent you a text too, Sam."

"So you all are texting one another in class?" Mr. Pell said.

"Sort of?" Sam said. Mr. Pell knew the notebooks weren't phones, didn't he? Sam was surprised by how many grown-ups found his notebooks confusing.

Mr. Pell scooped up the notebooks and took them over to the front of the room, where he dropped them all in his desk drawer. "You all can have these back when school is over," he said.

"But we might need them before then!" Marja said. "What are we supposed to do if Jackson decides to beat up Sam and Gavin and punch their teeth out?"

"What?" Mr. Pell turned to Sam and Gavin. "Guys? Care to explain?"

Sam shook his head. He did not care to explain. He'd come up with a great plan for *not* getting beat up, and now Marja had ruined it.

When Gavin didn't say anything either, Mr. Pell said, "You two stay in for recess. I think we need to have a talk."

Chapter Eleven

The Latest, Greatest Notebook Fad

"**Y**ou don't need to worry, Mr. Pell," Gavin said later that morning, when the rest of the class had gone to the playground for recess. "Sam has a really good plan."

Mr. Pell looked at Sam. "I assume this has something to do with the note Mr. Cameron sent the other day?"

"Kind of," Sam said. "It's because Jackson Grubb got in trouble and we didn't."

"And now we're in trouble with Jackson Grubb," Gavin added.

"But now we know how to get out of it," Sam said. "I've got a plan, just like Gavin said."

Sam explained to Mr. Pell about what happened at the school store and how they were going to annoy Jackson until he left them alone. When he was finished explaining, Mr. Pell smiled, which was good. But he also shook his head, which wasn't so good.

"You always come up with great plans, Sam," Mr. Pell said. "And this one might work, it's true. But I can't let somebody threaten you and not do anything about it."

"He didn't actually say he was going to punch us in the mouth," Sam said. "That's just what Gavin thinks he *might* do."

"Maybe not," Mr. Pell said. "But he did

threaten to make trouble for you. He's being a bully, Sam, and we don't allow that in our school."

"Did I mention we have a bodyguard?" Sam asked his teacher.

"The fact that you think you need a bodyguard doesn't make me feel any better about this situation," Mr. Pell said. "No, we need to sit down with Mr. Cameron and Jackson and talk this out."

Sam sighed. "I guess that's one way to pop the balloon," he said. "But it's not my favorite way."

"Why do you keep talking about balloons?" Gavin asked him. "Is it your birthday or something?"

"Why don't you guys head out to the playground and I'll go talk to Mr. Cameron?" Mr. Pell said. "Maybe we can set up a meeting for later this afternoon."

"I still think we should do your plan," Gavin whispered as they headed for the door. "If Jackson gets in more trouble, he'll just find sneakier ways to get us."

Why couldn't grown-ups understand that? Sam wondered as he followed Gavin into the hallway. They always wanted to talk about everything. They thought talking about things solved every single problem. Talking about things might solve *some* problems, Sam guessed, but it could also make some problems worse. Like *this* problem, for instance.

As Sam and Gavin got closer to the big field, Sam noticed something strange. Instead of running around and kicking a soccer ball, the members of the Barracudas were standing on the sideline, looking down at their hands. People on the other fifth-grade soccer team were yelling, "Are you guys going to play or what?"

"What are they doing?" Gavin asked, but Sam couldn't tell. All he knew is that it looked weird to see Janie Kramer and her friends standing still when they should be playing soccer.

Emily came over to where Sam and Gavin were standing. She was followed by Marja and Will. "They stole your idea, Sam," Emily said. "They're all texting."

"But Janie said she didn't have a— Oh." Sam looked closer at the Barracudas. They were all writing in little notebooks just like Sam's and passing them around. "That looks sort of weird."

"You started a fad, Sam!" Marja exclaimed. "I heard a bunch of kids say they were going to the school store first thing during lunch period to buy little notebooks like ours."

"I heard the school store was sold out of notebooks," Will said. "I also heard that somebody's mom is going to go to the mall, buy notebooks, and then bring them to school this afternoon."

"A mom is going to come to our school and sell notebooks?" Gavin asked. "Are moms allowed to do that? Could my mom come and sell pencils and erasers?"

"What I heard is that this mom is going to drop the notebooks off so her kid can sell them," Will said. "For a *dollar*."

"But the notebooks are only supposed

to cost fifty cents," Sam said. "A dollar's too much."

Will shrugged. "I guess some people don't mind as long as they can get a notebook. Now I wish I'd bought ten notebooks. I could make a fortune selling them to other people."

The recess monitors' whistles blew, but Sam noticed that hardly any of the Barracudas moved to go back inside. They were still busy writing messages in their notebooks and passing their notebooks around.

"The fifth graders are copying us!" Gavin said. "That's so cool!"

Sam wondered if the fifth graders knew they were copying his idea to use a notebook for a phone? Did they know they really needed at least three notebooks, four if they wanted to write stories they could read later? Maybe he could charge people a dollar to teach them the right way to make phones.

"I wonder when Mr. Pell is going to give our notebooks back," Emily said as they started walking toward the school entrance. "Because I just saw a red-crested woodpecker, and I wanted to send you guys a message about it."

"Aren't you telling us about it now?" Gavin said.

"Yes," Emily said. "But I'd still like to send you a message. Although maybe not in code—writing in code takes a really long time."

"It takes forever," Marja complained. "I'm only going to use secret codes when I have supersecret stuff."

When they got back to their classroom, Mr. Pell told everyone to take their writing notebooks out so they could work on their stories. Sam wanted to take his story notebook out of his back pocket so he could write some more about Frozen Fred, but he was afraid Mr. Pell might take it and put it in his drawer with the other notebooks. Sam took out his regular writing notebook instead and opened it to the first blank page. Maybe he could start a new story, one about a chicken that was really good at flying. As far as Sam could tell, chickens were terrible flyers. They could fly, but they just couldn't get very far off the ground.

He could call his main character Chester. Sam decided that Chester was the sort of chicken who watched other kinds of birds fly and wished he could fly as high as they did. This is going to be good, Sam thought as he leaned over his notebook to start writing his story. Maybe Chester practiced flying by jumping off the roof of his coop, which made his mom mad because she thought he was going to hurt himself.

Chester was the bravest chicken in his coop, Sam wrote. *The other chickens liked to stay on the ground, but not Chester. Chester always—*

"Sam and Gavin?"

Sam looked up. Mr. Pell was standing by the classroom door and motioning at him and Gavin to come over.

"Mr. Cameron just texted me," Mr. Pell told them when they reached the door. "He's ready to talk to you now."

"Will Jackson Grubb be there?" Sam asked, and Mr. Pell nodded.

"There's nothing to worry about," Mr. Pell said as they walked out into the hallway. "You guys are going to get everything worked out."

"I wish we could take Janie with us to this meeting," Gavin said as he and Sam started down the hallway. "I'd feel better if she were there."

Sam nodded. He wished they could take Janie, Annabelle, and Mr. Stockfish too. And all the chickens and his mom and dad.

That was the weird thing, Sam thought as he and Gavin trudged toward Mr. Cameron's office at the front of the school. He knew all sorts of people who would be happy to help. But you couldn't keep people with you everywhere you went, like they were notebooks you could pull out of your pocket whenever you needed them.

Sam glanced at Gavin. At least he had his best friend with him. That made him feel a little bit better. Which was good— since Sam was pretty sure his life was about to get a whole lot worse.

Chapter Twelve

Sam Graham, Research Man

When they reached the waiting room outside of Mr. Cameron's office, Jackson was already there, sitting in a chair by the window and looking at his phone.

Except that it wasn't a phone, Sam realized. It was a notebook.

"You're copying us too?" Gavin asked when he saw the notebook in Jackson's hand. "I don't think you should copy us if you're going to beat us up."

"I have no idea what you're talking about," Jackson said, not bothering to look up. "Everybody's got a notebook now. Some people have two."

"Sam has four notebooks," Gavin bragged. "That means he's four times better than you are."

Sam kept quiet. He was still waiting for Jackson to say whether or not he was going to beat them up.

"Boys?" Mr. Cameron stood at the door of his office. "Come on in and let's talk."

Sam waited for Jackson to whisper something mean in his ear, like *I'll give you something to talk about later*, but he didn't. He just put his notebook in his pocket and followed Mr. Cameron into his office.

"So, Jackson," Mr. Cameron began once

they all sat down. "Sam and Gavin here seem to think you're mad at them. Is that true?"

Jackson looked confused. "Why would I be mad? We had a misunderstanding, but that's over, right, guys?"

"But you told us that if you got in trouble, we'd get in trouble," Sam said. "You gave us a mean look through Mr. Pell's window."

"I did?" Jackson said. "That's not how I remember it. What I remember is saying I was sorry if I'd gotten you in trouble. And I've never looked at you after that."

Sam could feel his face get hot and his throat grow tight. Jackson Grubbs was lying! In the vice principal's office! Sam gripped the seat of his chair with both hands so he wouldn't start yelling.

"Sam? You look upset," Mr. Cameron said. "Do you want to say something?"

Sam shook his head. He couldn't talk. This was terrible!

"Sam's mad," Gavin said. "I can tell because we're best friends, and best friends know. If he starts talking, he'll probably cry, and he doesn't want to cry."

"Why is Sam mad?" Mr. Cameron said. He turned to Sam. "It's okay if you cry, Sam. You're among friends."

But Sam knew it wasn't okay. If he cried, Jackson Grubb would tell everyone, and people would call him a crybaby. So he just shook his head again.

"Sam's mad," Gavin said matter-of-factly, "because Jackson is lying."

"That's not true," Jackson said. He

sounded like he was talking to a three-year-old. "Why would I lie to a couple of first graders?"

"Second graders," Mr. Cameron corrected him. "And the question is whether or not you're lying to *me*, not to them."

That made Sam feel a little better. At least Mr. Cameron didn't believe every word that came out of Jackson's mouth was a fact. He took a deep breath and said, "We have a bodyguard. Why would we have a bodyguard if Jackson didn't tell us we were going to be in trouble if he got in trouble?"

"That's a good question," Mr. Cameron said. He turned to Jackson. "The fact that these boys feel the need for protection concerns me. Maybe there's been a misunderstanding, or maybe Sam and Gavin have a reason to be concerned. Either way, we need to solve this problem. Any ideas?"

Jackson shrugged. "Nope."

"Maybe Jackson could sign a paper saying he's not going to punch us in the mouth," Gavin said. "And you could make copies to send everyone in the school, so even if Jackson *wanted* to punch us in the mouth, he'd at least think about it first."

"Do you think it might embarrass Jackson if we did that?" Mr. Cameron asked.

Gavin nodded. "Yes! That's why it's such a great idea."

"I'd like to come up with a plan that doesn't embarrass anyone," Mr. Cameron said. "I think embarrassing people makes things worse. So here's what I want you boys to do. You're going to eat lunch in the library today, and together you're going to come up with a community project that all three of you do together—a project that helps the school."

"What?! That sort of feels like you're punishing us," Sam said, feeling angry but trying not to *sound* angry, which made his words come out a little trembly. "And Gavin and I didn't do anything wrong."

"You did something a little bit wrong, Sam," Mr. Cameron reminded him. "You shouldn't have taken the notebooks from the school store, even if you did pay for them. The only person allowed in the store is the person working there." Mr. Cameron looked at his watch. "Okay, it's almost lunchtime, so why don't you boys grab your lunches and head over to the library. Mrs. Haynie knows you're coming."

"This is going to be the worst lunch ever," Gavin whispered to Sam as they left Mr. Cameron's office. "I'll probably throw up halfway through."

Sam wasn't looking forward to lunch either. He didn't think he'd throw up, although he might if Gavin threw up first. But spending thirty minutes with Jackson Grubb was going to be no fun. Jackson would probably call them first-grade pipsqueaks and make fun of them because they couldn't write in cursive yet.

It turned out they would be eating lunch in the library conference room. Mrs. Haynie had put out a yellow tablecloth on the conference room table and set out a plate of cookies. "I'm going to close the door so you guys can talk without disturbing anyone," she said after Sam and Gavin sat down next to Jackson. "I know you're going to come up with some great ideas!"

Sam tried to smile at the librarian, because she was nice and he liked her. But he sort of wished she'd leave the door open.

"Okay, here's my idea for a school community project," Jackson started as soon as Mrs. Haynie left the room and closed the door. "I think we need a skateboard ramp. I know about twenty kids who would bring their boards to school every day if we had a ramp. I know I would."

"I bet the school wouldn't let us," Gavin said. "Too dangerous."

"Maybe," Jackson said. "But they've got one at my cousin's school. You can make them safe, and you can have rules, like everybody has to wear a helmet."

Sam blinked a couple times. Was this the same Jackson Grubb from the school store? From the window in the classroom door? From Mr. Cameron's office?

"Why are you acting like a regular person?" he asked. "And not like somebody who wants to beat us up?"

Jackson thought about this for a moment. "I was never going to beat you up. I don't beat up pipsqueaks, for one thing. I don't actually beat up anyone. I was just mad because I got in trouble—for something that was sort of your fault, just like Mr. Cameron said."

"It was a whole lot more your fault," Gavin pointed out. "You should have sold us the notebooks instead of being mean about it."

"I was hungry," Jackson said with a shrug. "And you were annoying me. Bad combo."

"So you're not going to beat us up?" Sam asked, just to make sure.

"Nope," Jackson said. "Not interested."

"No more scary faces at Mr. Pell's door?"

"That's all behind us now."

Sam let out a deep breath. Okay then. "We would have to do research first," Sam told Jackson, pulling out his information notebook and a pencil from his right back pocket. He wrote the word *research* at the top of a blank page. "If we could show that other schools have skateboard ramps and they're safe, maybe we could get one too."

"Sam's really good at doing research," Gavin told Jackson. "He can find out all that stuff in, like, five seconds."

"We'd need to to find out how much a skateboard ramp costs," Jackson said. He took a bite of his sandwich, swallowed, and then looked at Sam. "Could you find that out too?"

Sam nodded. "I think so. I can get my sister to help me."

"Cool, that's your job then," Jackson said. He pointed to Gavin. "Do you know what a petition is?"

"Maybe?" Gavin said. "Sort of?" He paused. "No, not really."

"A petition is a piece of paper that you get people to sign," Jackson said. "On top of the paper it would say something like 'We the people would like a skateboard ramp at our school.' You get, like, a hundred kids to sign it so that the principal knows we mean business. You think you can do that?"

"I'll get two hundred people to sign it," Gavin promised. "I'll get a thousand people. I'll get—"

"A hundred kids who go to this school

and know how to write their first and last names would be good," Jackson told him. "Okay, so then we have to come up with a fund-raising plan. Maybe we could do a bake sale or something. Or sell pencils with the school's name on them."

Sell pencils? Who wanted to buy a pencil? Sam thought. Pencils were boring. No, there was something else they could sell that Sam thought everyone would want to buy.

He leaned across the table toward Jackson Grubb. "I've got a plan."

"Sam's really good at plans," Gavin said.

"I'm the best at plans," Sam said. He was pretty sure he wasn't bragging when he said that either. He was pretty sure he was telling the truth.

Chapter Thirteen

Frozen Fred, the Skateboarding Waffle

"So how many notebooks did you sell today?" Mr. Stockfish asked, patting Leroy on the head. "As many as you sold yesterday?"

Sam pulled out his information notebook. "Yesterday we sold forty-seven," he reported. "Today we sold thirty-nine."

"Do you really think you're going to sell enough notebooks to buy a skateboard ramp?" Mr. Stockfish sounded doubtful.

"No, but that's okay," Sam said. "Because someone's dad who works for a lumber company is going to donate the wood for the ramp. And someone else's mom owns a hardware store, so she's going to donate the parts you need to hook everything together."

"Who's going to build the ramp?"

"A bunch of us kids and the vice principal," Sam told him. "Mr. Cameron used to be a skateboarding champion. Yesterday he brought his trophies to school."

"I wonder if Leroy would enjoying riding on a skateboard?" Mr. Stockfish picked up his chicken and looked her in the eye. "She might like a nice roll down the block."

Chickens on skateboards! That gave Sam an idea. He pulled out his camera notebook and started to draw. Most of the pictures in his camera notebook were of chickens and chicken stuff, he realized. Maybe one day he'd grow up to be a chicken photographer.

Sam was excited about the skateboard ramp. First of all, Mr. Cameron had been so happy that Sam, Gavin, and Jackson had come up with a community project idea that he made them team leaders, which meant they were the bosses. Second, now Sam and Gavin were Jackson's new best friends, or at least his new second-grade best friends. Third, Sam's dad said he would get Sam a skateboard so he could use the ramp, and Sam's mom said she'd get him a helmet, because wearing a helmet was going to be one of the rules for skateboarding at school.

"I wonder if skateboarding is going to be my new thing," Sam said to Mr. Stockfish as they got ready to walk home. "I might be really good at it, and now it's going to be in the Olympics."

"Skateboarding is a good way to break your arm," Mr. Stockfish said. He set down Leroy and pushed himself up from his chair. "So maybe wearing a cast can be your new thing."

After Sam walked Mr. Stockfish back to his house, he went home, wishing it was dinnertime already, because he was hungry. His dad was working in his office off the kitchen, so Sam went to ask if he could have a frozen waffle.

"Just one," Sam said. "I promise it won't spoil my appetite."

"I guess one is okay," his dad said. "Are

you sure you don't want to toast it?"

"Toasted waffles taste weird," Sam told his dad. "They're mushy on the inside."

"Not if you toast them long enough," Sam's dad said, following Sam into the kitchen. "And they're nice and crispy on the outside. And when you toast your waffle, you can put butter on top and it melts . . ."

Sam opened the freezer door. "Would you like a waffle too?"

"Yeah, come to think of it, I would. Do you mind popping one into the toaster for me?"

Sam's dad sat down at the kitchen table. Sam got out two waffles and put one in the toaster and pushed the on button.

"Did you ever finish writing your waffle story?" Sam's dad asked.

"I haven't had time," Sam said. "I've been busy researching skateboard ramps and selling notebooks."

"So your phone idea really caught on, huh?" Sam's dad sounded proud. "Notebooks are better than phones, in my opinion. They make you more creative—"

Sam's dad was interrupted by a ping. It was his phone.

"I should probably check this out," he said. "I'm expecting a text from work."

Sam thought the good thing about having a notebook phone instead of a phone-phone was that notebook phones never pinged. More importantly, they never got in the way of eating waffles. He sat down at the table with his frozen waffle and took out his story notebook. What was going to happen to Frozen Fred next, now that he was out of the freezer? he wondered. Where would he go and how would he get there?

Sam bit into his waffle. It was like eating a waffle popsicle, he thought. All that was missing was a stick.

And all Frozen Fred was missing was a skateboard! Maybe there was a kid in Fred's house who had a skateboard and left it by the refrigerator one day. When Fred rolled out of the freezer, he could fall on the skateboard and roll away! But what if the family had a dog? And the dog started chasing after the skateboard because he wanted to eat Fred?

Sam had a feeling his story about Fred was about to turn into a whole book about Fred. The title could be *Frozen Fred, the Skateboarding Waffle*.

"I'm going upstairs," Sam called to his dad. "Don't forget your waffle!"

When he got to his room, Sam laid out his four notebooks on his desk. All the information in the world was right in front of him. Okay, maybe not all the information. Sam knew he could find more facts, pictures, and stories on a real phone than in his notebooks. But the one thing a phone wouldn't have was Sam's stories and Sam's pictures. Maybe someday he'd ask Annabelle how to upload things to the computer so he could share his stories and pictures with a thousand people all at once.

But for now, Sam liked having everything on his desk where he could see it whenever he wanted, without having to press a single button. He sat down and reached into the top desk drawer for his colored pencils. First he was going to practice drawing waffles. After that, he was going to write some more of Frozen Fred's story.

And then maybe he'd ask if they could have waffles for dinner. Maybe even frozen waffles on sticks.

Sam got hungry just thinking about it.

Acknowledgments

The author would like to thank her editor, the indomitable Caitlyn Dlouhy, and the very kind and capable Alex Borbolla. Cheers to ace publisher Justin Chanda and the world's best copy editor, Clare McGlade. Thanks as always to Sam supporter Xyrell Goldston, champion reader. Finally, she owes a debt of gratitude to her family, Clifton, Jack, Will, and Travis the Dog.

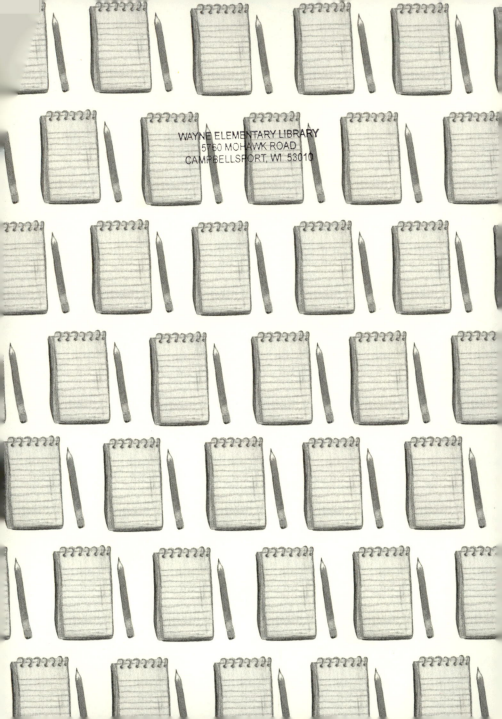